THE COMIC

Anupa Lal has writte ... ...
These include a rete ... ... books of
poems, and translations of several short stories by the noted
Hindi writer Premchand as well as his last novel *Godan*.

The Comic Capers of Sheikh Chilli

Retold by
Anupa Lal

SCHOLASTIC
New York Toronto London Auckland Sydney
New Delhi Hong Kong

Published by Scholastic India Pvt. Ltd.
A subsidiary of Scholastic Inc., New York, 10012 (USA).
Publishers since 1920, with international operations in Canada, Australia, New Zealand, the United Kingdom, Mexico, India, Argentina and Hong Kong.

For information regarding permission, write to:
Scholastic India Pvt. Ltd.
Golf View Corporate Tower-A, 3rd Floor,
DLF Phase-V, Gurgaon 122002 (India)

Typeset by Mantra Virtual Services Pvt Ltd

First edition: September 2007
Reprinted: September, October 2007, September, November 2009,
April, July 2010, May 2012, October February 2014

ISBN-13: 978-81-7655-847

Printed at: Ram Printograph (India), Delhi

Contents

Introduction   *vii*

A Tumbler of Oil   1

The Soldier   6

The Feverish Sickle   10

The Watermelon and the Thieves   15

Midnight Adventures 1   20

Midnight Adventures 2   26

The Nightmare   33

The Horse's Egg   37

The Kazi 1   42

The Kazi 2   49

Half of That   56

In the City   60

Visit to the In-laws   66

The Guest Who Would Not Leave   71

The Black Thread   76

The Courier   80

The Bottle of Oil   84

The Leopard   88

Chhotey Nawab and the Liar   91

The Capture   95

Introduction

Who was Sheikh Chilli? No one really knows, but stories about him have amused generations of readers both in India and Pakistan. He has been portrayed as a fool, a simpleton, who couldn't do anything right! And as an inveterate daydreamer, building castles in the air.

Born a sheikh, one of the four major Muslim sub-castes, Sheikh Chilli was the son of a poor widow. Little else is known about him, making it impossible to separate fact from fiction in the stories that feature him.

According to one account, he was born in

Baluchistan, in Pakistan; moved to what is now Haryana, worked for many years for the Nawab of Jhajjar, and died in Kurukshetra, where the tomb of Sheikh Chilli can still be seen. It is said that in his later years, he became a fakir. The 'Chilli' part of his name could refer to his having performed a *chilla*, i.e. forty days of continuous prayer. Whether this account is historically accurate or not, is of course, debatable.

Sheikh Chilli may not have had the wit of Birbal or Tenali Raman, two other 'comic' characters well known in the subcontinent; but to see him in his childhood and youth, merely as an object of ridicule, would be doing an injustice to the complexity of his character.

Sheikh Chilli was an innocent, whose attempts to conform to the dictates of society might have been laughable, but they were, for the most part, well-meant. Devoid of envy or bitterness, guileless and helpful by nature, he was seldom cunning enough to be called a shirker. He was a daydreamer—yes, at odds with reality. But who does not often dream of better times ahead?

The fact that there is a bit of Sheikh Chilli in each of us, accounts, perhaps, for his long-standing popularity!

A Tumbler of Oil

It was a clear windy day. Just the weather to fly a kite! Sheikh Chilli was on the roof of his house, kite firmly in hand, squinting up towards the sky, watching his red and green kite soar higher and higher. If only I could be tiny enough to sit on my kite and fly off into the sky ... thought Sheikh Chilli.

But he was rudely shaken out of his innocent reverie by the voice of his mother. 'Beta where are you?' she asked, shading her eyes as she tried to look up at him.

'Coming Ammi,' answered Sheikh Chilli sadly. Slowly he brought his kite back to earth and ran downstairs. Sheikh was his mother's only child, her only family after the death of her husband, and she loved him dearly.

Sheikh Chilli's mother handed him an empty tumbler and an eight-anna coin and said, 'Beta, get me eight annas worth of mustard oil in this. Bring the oil carefully and hurry back.' And then she added her customary warning, 'Don't start dreaming on the way, do you hear me?'

'Yes, Ammi,' said Sheikh. 'Don't look so worried. You look less beautiful when you worry.'

'Less beautiful!' his mother said in mock exasperation. 'Where have I the time or the money to look beautiful? Go on, you flatterer. Hurry to the market and get me the oil.'

Sheikh ran all the way to the market. Normally, he would have ambled along but now since his ammi had told him to hurry, so he did.

Arriving at the store almost completely out of breath, Sheikh Chilli handed the tumbler and the eight anna coin to the shopkeeper, Lala Teli Ram. 'Lalaji, Ammi wants eight annas worth of mustard oil,' he panted.

The shopkeeper measured out eight annas worth of oil from a large tin and began pouring it into the tumbler till it was full.

'This tumbler can only contain seven annas worth of oil,' he said to Sheikh. 'What shall I do with the rest? Have you got another container or shall I return an anna?'

Sheikh was in a fix. His ammi had not given him another tumbler or told him to bring back any money. What should he do? Then he had a brainwave! There was a hollow space in the outer bottom of the tumbler. The extra oil would fit in there!

Happily he turned the tumbler full of oil upside down! All the oil flowed out. Sheikh pointed to the hollow space in the tumbler. 'Pour the rest of the oil in here,' he said.

Lala Teli Ram was stupefied. Shaking his head in disbelief, the Lala did as he was told. Sheikh held the tumbler carefully and set off homewards, quite oblivious of the titters of those who had seen the entire incident.

Sheikh's mother was washing clothes when he arrived. 'Where is the rest of the oil?' she demanded, looking with great bewilderment at the small quantity of oil at the bottom of the tumbler.

'Here!' said Sheikh, turning the tumbler the right way up and losing the rest of the oil as well!

'It was here Ammijan, I promise. I saw Lalaji pouring it in. Where has it gone?'

3

'Into the ground, along with your wits!' said his mother angrily. 'Is there no limit to your foolishness?'

Sheikh was most offended. 'I did exactly what you told me to,' he protested. 'You told me to bring back eight annas worth of oil in this tumbler, and I did. You didn't tell me what to do if the tumbler was too small. You gave me a small tumbler and now you are getting angry. Don't get angry Ammi. You look less beautiful when you—'

'I'll beautify you if you don't get out of my sight for a while!' said his ammi, picking up a broom that was lying nearby. 'There is a limit to my patience, even if there isn't to your stupidity!'

Sheikh ran up to the roof with his kite. Wearily, his mother went back to washing clothes. She would have to go to the market herself to get more oil. Sheikh had wasted precious time and precious money. And yet she knew what a loving and obedient son he was.

A short while later, someone thumped on the outer door of the house. It was Lala Teli Ram's young son with a bottle of oil. 'This is yours, Buaji,' he said. 'My father sent it. When Sheikh Bhaiyya turned the tumbler of oil upside down, fortunately the oil fell back into the tin! Where is Bhaiyya? He had promised to teach me to fly a kite.'

Sheikh's mother was enormously relieved. 'He is

on the roof. Go up, beta,' she said, taking the oil and patting the boy's cheek. She went back to her work with a smile on her lips. Allah had not forgotten this poor widow!

The Soldier

'Keep your eyes on the ground, and your feet on the
road … keep your eyes on the ground and your feet
on the road … keep your feet on your eyes and the
road on your ground…' Sheikh Chilli was so intent
on repeating his mother's warning to him, lest he
forget it, that he did not realise that he had walked
right off the road and straight into a tree!

'Uff!' he exclaimed, rubbing his smarting nose.
What was the tree doing in the middle of the road?
Ammi had told him to walk in the middle of the

road until he reached the house of the tailor.

'Don't start looking around as you always do or you'll never reach!' Ammi had said sternly. 'Do you hear me? Keep your eyes on the ground, and your feet …'

Banging into a tree was not part of her instructions, Sheikh mused sadly as he tried to straighten the imaginary bend in his nose. And then he discovered where he was. In the middle of a field! And, as for the road it was nowhere in sight. His feet must have gone in one direction and the road in the other. He glowered at his feet but that didn't help.

Well, Sheikh Chilli thought, now that the tree was right in front of him, he may as well climb it and see if he could spot the road he should have been on. Clambering on to a branch, he looked around and spotted the road far away to the right. Sheikh caught hold of one of the lower branches of the tree and was about to jump down when he saw a well just beneath him! How beautiful the water looked, deep down in the well, glinting in the sunlight.

Sheikh hung from the branch, swinging happily in the breeze. He closed his eyes and imagined he was whizzing through the air on the back of his favourite kite.

Dhuk! Dharrak! Dhuk! Dharrak!

His pet elephant was racing down the path below

him with Ammi seated on his back. She was dressed in red satin as befitted the mother of Sultan Sheikh Chilli!

Dhuk! Dharrak! Dhuk! Dharrak!

Sheikh opened his eyes. There was no sign of his elephant and he was still dangling above the well! But a soldier on horseback was galloping towards him on one of the paths that criss-crossed the field.

'Don't panic!' the soldier shouted. 'I'll save you! Don't panic!' He came as close to the well as he could. Sheikh looked at him with great interest. He had a handsome moustache curling at the edges. The rest of him, from turban to boots, was very dusty.

'Stay calm,' said the horseman, 'and listen to me carefully. My horse will jump across this well. As I pass under you I'll catch hold of your legs. At that moment, let go of the branch and you'll be safe on my horse with me. Have you understood?'

Sheikh nodded vigorously. The soldier retreated a few paces, then raced towards the well and jumped smartly across it! As he passed below Sheikh, the soldier grabbed his legs. But Sheikh hung on to the branch from which he was dangling! The horse cleared the well but his master was left dangling below Sheikh.

'Why didn't you let go?' demanded the surprised soldier, craning his neck to glare at Sheikh.

Sheikh was equally surprised! 'I'm sorry,' he said, 'but I really don't know why!'

He spread out his arms to show his bewilderment. And down he and the soldier plunged, straight into the well!

SPLASH!

The horse galloped off in alarm. Farmers in a nearby field brought back the horse and hauled Sheikh and the angry soldier out of the well.

Luckily, his ammi wasn't angry when Sheikh returned home wet and muddy, without having delivered her message to the tailor.

'Just as well you didn't reach his house,' she said, helping Sheikh out of his wet clothes, 'because I met him right here. But there is no well on the way to his house, so how did you—'

The well had suddenly appeared, Sheikh remembered. So had the tree. And the soldier on horseback. What an adventure! Sheikh smiled as he remembered it and picked up his kite.

'Ammijan,' he said, as he ran up the stairs to the roof, 'when I grow up, I'm going to have the biggest moustache you've ever seen!'

The Feverish Sickle

One morning, dressed in her Sunday best, Sheikh Chilli's mother was preparing to leave for Fatima Bibi's house. Sheikh's mother earned a living by doing odd jobs for the wealthy families of the village.

'Beta Sheikh,' she said, 'I am going to Fatima Bibi's house to help with the preparations for her daughter's wedding. I'll be back at night, perhaps with some sweets for my precious son. Fatima Bi is a generous soul!

Then, speaking very, very slowly so that Sheikh

would not miss a word of what she was going to say, she said, 'Take this sickle … go into the jungle … cut lots of grass for our neighbour's cow … don't dawdle on the way and don't daydream while you are working. You might cut yourself with the sickle if you are not careful.'

'Inshallah, both you and I may earn well today,' she added wistfully, without a pause.

'Don't worry about me, Ammijan,' Sheikh reassured her. He set off cheerfully for the jungle, wondering what his ammi would bring back from Fatima Bi's house. Would it be beautiful, soft, brown, juicy gulab jamuns, which he had once tasted? Thinking of them almost brought the taste back!

'Stop it!' he said to himself sternly. 'Ammi told you not to daydream.'

Sheikh reached the jungle and set to work with gusto. By lunchtime he had cut a lot of grass. He made a big bundle of it and brought it home. It was only after he had deposited the grass in his neighbour's yard, earned a few annas, come home and had his lunch of thick rotis and chutney, that he remembered that he had left the sickle in the jungle. He hurried back. The sickle was lying where he had left it. The blazing sun had heated the blade so much that Sheikh recoiled when he touched it. What had happened to the sickle? He was staring at it with a puzzled frown when Lallan, a boy who lived in his neighbourhood, happened to pass by.

'Mian, what are you staring at?' he asked.

'At my sickle. Something has happened to it. It's so hot!'

'Hai Ram! It's got fever!' said Lallan, laughing inwardly at Sheikh's ignorance. 'You should take it to the hakim. But wait. I know exactly what Hakimji prescribes for high fever. Come with me.'

Holding the sickle gingerly by its wooden handle, Lallan led Sheikh to a nearby well. Tying the sickle to a long rope attached to the well, he dangled it in the cool water.

'Leave it like this and go home,' he said to Sheikh. 'Come back just before dark. The sickle's fever will have gone by then.'

'And so will the sickle, you fool!' he added silently. 'I'll hide it or sell it so that your mother gives you a good beating for losing it!'

'Believe me Mian,' he said aloud. 'This is the best remedy for fever!'

Sheikh Chilli believed him and went home. He fell asleep and awoke as the sun was setting. 'I'd better fetch the sickle before Ammi comes home,' he thought. 'Its fever must have gone by now.'

He set off for the well. On the way was Lallan's house. As he passed it, he heard someone moaning inside. Sheikh went in. Lallan's grandma lay tossing and turning on a string cot in the empty courtyard. Sheikh approached her and got a fright. Her skin was burning hot. She had high fever and there was no one to help her but him. Then a happy realisation dawned on him. Thanks to Lallan, he now knew how to take care of a fever!

Sheikh hoisted the old lady carefully on his back and began walking with her towards the well.

'Mian, where are you taking Lallan's grandma?' called out a neighbour.

'For treatment,' Sheikh replied. 'She has high fever.'

Lallan and his father had gone to the hakim to fetch some medicine for the old lady. They returned home to find her missing! As they ran up and down the lane looking for her, they met the neighbour who had called out to Sheikh Chilli.

Lallan turned pale as he realised where Sheikh was headed with his burden! He ran towards the well, with his father in hot pursuit. When they arrived on the scene, Sheikh was attempting to tie the old lady with the rope, having already retrieved his sickle (which incidentally, Lallan had had no time to steal).

'You fool, what are you doing?' shouted Lallan's father, pushing Sheikh away and untying his unconscious mother.

'Chacha, she has high fever!' Sheikh said excitedly. 'Tie her up and put her in the well. That's the best treatment for fever. Lallan told me.'

Lallan's father turned on his son like a tiger. 'What mischief have you been up to now?' he shouted. 'You rogue! I'll deal with you later! Now help me get your grandma home and then run for the hakim, if you value your life, you scoundrel!'

Lallan's grandma recovered in a few days while Lallan got the thrashing of his life from his father. Meanwhile, Sheikh's ammi did not know whether to laugh or cry when she heard the whole story! As Sheikh enjoyed the juicy gulab jamuns she had brought, she tried her best to explain to him why the sickle had got hot and why dunking someone in a well was really not the best thing to do for high fever!

The Watermelon and the Thieves

It must be a large watermelon. A large red watermelon. A round, red and juicy watermelon. Juicy, red and round … round, red and juicy. Sheikh Chilli could not get the watermelon out of his mind. And because he could not get the watermelon out of his mind, he could not fall asleep. The object of his fantasy—the watermelon —was the one that had been given to Sheikh's ammi by Fatima Bibi, and which she had left behind in her house that evening.

For the last week Ammi had been going to Fatima Bi's house for several hours everyday to help with the preparations for the marriage of Fatima Bi's eldest daughter. And everyday Ammi had brought back something for Sheikh that Fatima Bi had given her. The first day it had been juicy gulab jamuns, then some kheer, then a bunch of bananas. Today it was a big watermelon. Sheikh's mouth watered at the thought of it! Ammi had found it too heavy to carry, and had left it in the courtyard of Fatima Bi's house, thinking that Sheikh could fetch it in the morning. But Sheikh Chilli wanted it now. Now! said his hungry stomach. NOW!

By midnight, Sheikh could not hold himself back any longer. He had to have the watermelon. So he got up from his bed. Ammi was sound asleep. He tiptoed to the door and left the house quietly and walked to Fatima Bi's house through the dark, deserted lanes of the village. He jumped over the low wall surrounding the courtyard and there it was— his precious watermelon, lying on top of a pile of coal-filled sacks. He was just about to pick it up and leave, when he heard voices inside the house. Who could it be? The house was supposed to be empty. The entire family had gone to attend a function in the next village. Perhaps they had come back early. But then why would their front door be locked from outside? Sheikh was figuring this out when he heard approaching footsteps.

'Hai Ram!' moaned a voice he recognised as Lallan's. 'I'll kill that idiot Sheikh Chilli! Because of him my father thrashed me so hard that every bone in my body still aches! And now I've cut my hand, crawling through a window with broken glass.'

'Stop moaning!' hissed a voice Sheikh did not recognise. He hid behind the sacks of coal just as two figures came into view. Sheikh peered at them through a gap in the sacks. With Lallan was a mean-eyed stranger Sheikh Chilli had seen loitering in the bazaar. Lallan was carrying a bag full of something.

'Hurry up,' said the stranger. 'Let's divide the loot.'

To Sheikh's horror, the stranger came right up to the pile of sacks and sat down with his back against them. He grabbed the bag from Lallan and poured its contents on the ground. Necklaces, bangles of gold and silver, silver glasses and gold coins gleamed in the pale moonlight. Sheikh gaped at all the things he knew Fatima Bi had collected for her daughter's marriage. His ammi had described them to him. And now these two were going to steal them all!

'You've taken more than half the stuff!' protested Lallan weakly as the stranger pushed a small amount of the loot towards him.

'Be grateful you're getting this much!' growled

the stranger. 'Without me you wouldn't have had the nerve to rob this house!'

'It used to be haunted,' whispered Lallan, looking around him uneasily. 'Some people say it still is!'

'Then let's go before the ghost gets us!' The stranger grinned wickedly. 'If you want a bigger share of the loot, you can take that watermelon!'

He began pushing three quarters of the gold and silver back into the bag. Pocketing the rest and muttering to himself, Lallan stood up and tried to take the watermelon. But behind the sacks Sheikh Chilli had also stood up and was holding on to his watermelon with all his might! As his fingers touched Sheikh's, Lallan got the shock of his life!

'Ghost!' he quavered. 'Gh … Ghost!'

Sheikh leaned against the sacks and held on desperately to his watermelon. Two of the sacks toppled over and fell on Lallan and the stranger. Lallan threw all caution to the winds.

'Ghost!' he yelled loudly.

'Ghost!' yelled Sheikh Chilli, equally terrified. 'Ghost! Thief! Ghost!'

Before the two thieves had a chance to escape, a crowd had gathered near the house. Covered with coal dust, the two thieves were led away to the police station, with Lallan still muttering, 'Ghost! Ghost!'

One of the neighbours stood guard over the

almost-stolen valuables till Fatima Bibi and her family returned. Sheikh was escorted home like a hero, clutching his precious watermelon!

Midnight Adventures 1

Sheikh Chilli lay on his bed, gazing up at the stars. It was a beautiful summer night—too beautiful to waste sleeping! His mother lay asleep in the courtyard but Sheikh had dragged his bed to the edge of the fields. The night wind was cool, the stars twinkled and Sheikh smiled a smile of pure pleasure. Life was good …

Just then low voices broke the quiet of the night. Sheikh sat up and looked around. Two figures were crossing the first field. One was tall and upright, with a stylish, swaggering walk. The other figure was short and slight, hurrying to keep up with his companion.

'Veeru Bhaiyya and Buddhu!' breathed Sheikh Chilli and his eyes shone. Sheikh considered Veeru the most handsome man in the village. He had a fine moustache, flashing eyes, a deep voice and a muscular body. He was a champion wrestler, a champion kite-flier and Sheikh's idol. Buddhu was Veeru's shadow.

Sheikh got off his bed and ran up to the two figures. 'Veeru Bhaiyya, where are you going? Tell me please,' he panted.

'Sheikh! I thought you were a ghost!' Veeru grinned. He twirled the left end of his moustache. 'Buddhu and I are going to fly kites.'

'At this time? You're joking!' protested Sheikh. 'Veeru Bhaiyya, can I come with you wherever you're going? Please!'

'There's nowhere to go and nothing to do!' Veeru said gloomily, picking up a bare branch from the ground.

'Nothing!' echoed Buddhu, equally gloomily.

'This village is a dead place!' Veeru thwacked the air so hard with the branch that Buddhu jumped. Veeru grinned. 'We are going to rob somebody. Want to come along?'

'Yes,' said Sheikh at once. To share any adventure with Veeru, even a robbery, was a chance not to be missed!

'Who are we going to rob, Veeru Bhaiyya?' Sheikh whispered as they walked silently through the village. At that moment they were passing the house of fat Dhondu, the drummer. The sound of Dhondu's rich, bubbly snores filled the air.

'Come on,' said Veeru. 'Let's give the old pot-belly something to snore about!'

'Oh yes!' whispered Sheikh excitedly.

'Dhondu! Pot-belly Dhondu! Hee hee!' giggled Buddhu.

'SHHH!' Veeru said fiercely.

'Shhh!' repeated Buddhu meekly.

His heart thumping, Sheikh Chilli crept behind Veeru and Buddhu into Dhondu's house. The front door was not bolted. Dhondu was asleep in the corner of a large room, his big stomach rising and falling as he snored. Veeru, Buddhu and Sheikh moved around the room like shadows. Dhondu's drum stood beneath the window. Sheikh was drawn to it like iron to a magnet. The smooth surface of the dholak shone in the moonlight. Sheikh touched it lightly with his fingers. Then before he knew what he was doing, he hit it hard!

DUMMMMM! Boomed the drum.

Dhondu woke up with a start and fell off his bed. He looked at the frozen figures in the room and started yelling. Veeru ran out of the door, cursing under his breath. Buddhu ran behind him and Sheikh ran after them, the mighty boom of the dholak echoing pleasantly in his ears. What a magnificent instrument it was and how lucky Dhondu was to own it, he thought as he ran. If he had a dholak like that he would climb the highest hill near the village at daybreak and bang on the dholak till nightfall.

Sheikh bumped into Buddhu, stopped and looked around him. They had reached the edge of the field close to his home. Veeru glared at Sheikh. Sheikh stopped smiling. He opened his mouth to say something but Veeru turned away, spat angrily on the ground and stomped off. Buddhu too spat on the ground angrily and followed Veeru.

Sheikh stood looking after them sadly. 'Veeru Bhaiyya is annoyed with me,' he thought. 'I banged on the dholak and spoilt the robbery. But that dholak! O! What a lovely thing to own!' With a sigh of longing, Sheikh Chilli went home and fell fast asleep.

He slept soundly the next few nights, waking only at daybreak when his mother called him to draw water from the well. But the fifth night after his expedition with Veeru and Buddhu, he found himself wide-awake at midnight. He was trying to count the stars when to his great delight he heard voices and saw two familiar figures crossing the field. Excited at the prospect of another adventure, Sheikh ran after them.

Veeru turned as Sheikh reached him. 'Oho! It's the dholak champion!' he said dryly but his eyes were smiling. 'How did you know we were going to cross this field tonight? Have you become an astrologer as well as a dholak champion?'

Sheikh felt very happy. So this was to be the second adventure! Good! He fell into step with Veeru and Buddhu. Not a word was spoken as they walked along. Sheikh did not know where they were going, nor did he care. It was enough to be sharing a midnight jaunt with them!

Soon they were outside Kaano's house. Kaano, as she was known throughout the village, was a one-eyed, bad-tempered old woman, who was fond of nobody. Veeru, Buddhu and Sheikh looked at one another. Then all three crept into the courtyard where old Kaano lay asleep on a sagging bed. Veeru went quietly around the house, but all the doors and windows seemed bolted.

'Miser!' he muttered. 'What is she scared of?'

'Of us!' giggled Buddhu.

'Shh!' hissed Veeru and began examining the windows once again. Sheikh saw a pot on the earthen fireplace in a corner of the courtyard. It was full of warm kheer. Suddenly he felt very hungry. He picked up a ladle lying near the pot, scooped out a portion of the rice pudding, dipped in a finger and licked it.

'Pphuhh!' Sheikh screwed up his face and spat out the kheer. It was sugarless and tasted of burnt milk! He glared at the old woman snoring gently with her mouth open, crept over to her with the ladle and poured some of the burnt kheer into her mouth.

'Glugg!' Kaano choked and coughed, and awoke with a start. 'Hai! Hai!' she screamed. 'Don't hurt me!'

Veeru grabbed Sheikh and dragged him out of the courtyard. They ran down the lane with Buddhu behind them, panting and giggling. Kaano's cries faded into the distance. They were nearing Sheikh's house when Veeru stopped running and let go of his arm. There was a moment of uncomfortable silence.

'Idiot! If you come near me again Sheikh Chilli, I'll break your leg! Understand?' Veeru's eyes flashed fire. Sheikh hung his head and crossed his feet.

'Not just one leg, both your legs!' said Buddhu, trying to look as fierce as Veeru. 'Remember that!'

Sheikh walked home with a heavy heart and the awful taste of burnt kheer in his mouth. He rinsed his mouth thoroughly and fell into an uneasy slumber. The rest of the night he was haunted by dreams of Kaano chasing him around the field, brandishing a ladle and mouthing curses.

Midnight Adventures 2

Several nights went by. Sheikh slept fitfully, his ears straining for sounds of Veeru and Buddhu on yet another excursion. But all was quiet and peaceful. He had almost given up hope when one night he saw the two familiar figures crossing the field again. His heart jumped with joy! But Sheikh knew better than to approach them. Veeru was still furious. He had seen Sheikh in the bazaar one morning and glared at him. Sheikh waited till the two figures had gone ahead and then followed them as noiselessly as he could. Every now and then he hid behind a tree, fearful that Veeru might look back. But he didn't.

Sheikh began to enjoy himself. He walked on tiptoe, sometimes putting a finger on his lips, sometimes darting frightened looks right and left and sometimes even pretending to shiver!

Veeru and Buddhu seemed to be going on forever. Most of the houses in the village had been left behind. Suddenly the two stopped and Veeru looked around carefully. Sheikh had hidden himself behind a tree. Satisfied that no one had seen them, Veeru entered a courtyard, followed by Buddhu. Sheikh crept up after them, tingling with curiosity. It was the house of Bhiku Ram, a trader and money-lender. Bhiku Ram was one of the richest men in the village. He was also greedy and ruthless. Sheikh knew that Bhiku Ram's wife and children were away for a fortnight and that he was alone in the house.

Sheikh peeped into the courtyard. Bhiku Ram was fast asleep. Veeru and Buddhu had managed to push open a window. As Sheikh watched, Buddhu climbed in and the next minute he opened the front door softly for Veeru. Sheikh's heart was beating so loudly he was sure Bhiku Ram could hear it! He longed to follow Veeru in, but restrained himself. Nothing must interfere with Veeru's robbery this time! And who deserved to be robbed more than Bhiku Ram whose very livelihood, he had heard his ammi say, was robbing the poor?

Veeru and Buddhu came quietly out of the house. Both carried bulging sacks. Bhiku Ram was still asleep. So the robbery had been successful! Now he, Sheikh Chilli, must do his bit. He looked around and his eyes met Veeru's. Veeru stopped for a second, then turned and went out of the courtyard. Sheikh snatched up a small tandoor and a rope and hurried after him.

They had walked a fair distance before Veeru stopped under a large, leafy tree and waited for Sheikh to catch up. 'Hmm! So you decided to come along again?' he asked. 'Let's see what the dholak champion has brought away from Bhiku Ram's house.'

Sheikh eagerly held out the tandoor and rope for Veeru's inspection. As he did so, the three of them heard the sound of galloping horses. Veeru looked around. There was nowhere for them to hide.

'Quick! Climb up!' he urged the others. Buddhu was already swinging himself and his sack up into the branches of the tree. Veeru followed with his sack, leaning down to give Sheikh a helping hand as he struggled up, clasping the tandoor and rope to his chest.

'Why don't you leave them on the ground, you fool?' Veeru hissed. Sheikh shook his head firmly and continued to climb. A few moments later, three horsemen galloped into view and stopped under that very tree. Sheikh peered down at them. They had cloth around their faces and only their glittering eyes were visible. Daggers hung by their sides.

'Bandits!' Sheikh's mind whispered and he trembled. The tallest bandit pulled out his dagger and plunged it into the tree with a triumphant laugh.

'That was a clean job!' he exulted, untying the cloth from his face. His companions also untied their masks. The three men dismounted and squatted on the ground, a white bundle between them. 'That fool of a snake charmer was half dead from fright already! My knife didn't have much work to do. But who would have thought a dried-up stick like him would have so much gold and silver! He must have earned a lot in the city, the cunning fellow!'

'Shh!' one of the other robbers cautioned him. 'You always overdo things. What was the need to kill the old man? May God protect us from his spirit!'

'And from his snakes! They might decide to seek revenge too, who knows?' The tall robber laughed, a little uneasily. The white bundle was open now and Sheikh gasped as he saw silver anklets and amulets, gold coins, bangles and necklaces shining in the pale moonlight. It was the second time he had seen such wealth. The first time had been when Lallan and the stranger had tried to rob Fatima Bibi.

'Hai Ram! A snake!' One of the robbers was on his feet, staring terrified at something long and thin slithering down the tree.

Sheikh's heart missed a beat. A snake in the tree! What if it bit one of them? Veeru's foot in his ear made him look up. Veeru was making violent signs towards the tandoor and the rope that Sheikh was clutching. Sheikh found only the last bit of rope still in his grasp. Where was the rest? Good heavens! It had slithered down the tree and the bandits had mistaken it for a snake! Laughter filled Sheikh like air in a balloon. He bent down to peer at the robbers who were huddled together, staring at the 'snake'. For a moment Sheikh wondered if the rope had indeed magically turned into a snake! He pulled the 'snake' up a little and suddenly lost his balance on the branch. As he flung out a hand to steady himself, the tandoor slipped from his grasp.

'Oh!' gasped Sheikh, glancing up at Veeru. The tandoor plunged through the leaves, landed on the ground in front of the robbers with a sound like a thunderclap and exploded into a thousand pieces!

The panicky bandits froze in fright. Then they scrambled madly onto their horses, pushing each other in their haste, and galloped off into the night.

It was so sudden that Sheikh Chilli wasn't sure what had happened. He gazed after the fleeing robbers with his mouth open. Then Veeru's hand fell on his shoulder and his teeth flashed in a wide, warm smile.

'Shabash Sheikh! Well done!' said Veeru. 'You really are a champion! Your precious tandoor made the robbers run like rabbits! Come on, let's get off this tree! I feel as stiff as an old man! Come on Buddhu!'

The robbers had left behind the bundle of stolen gold and silver. Buddhu snatched it up gleefully and handed it to Veeru. For a long moment Veeru looked at the bundle in his hand and then at the things they had stolen from Bhiku Ram.

'What are you going to do with so much gold and silver, Veeru Bhaiyya?' asked Sheikh. 'Will you keep it or sell it?'

Veeru shook his head. 'It's all going back where it came from.'

'What?' cried Buddhu and Sheikh in astonishment.

'We are not robbers,' said Veeru, shrugging his shoulders restlessly. 'We stole—I don't know why— maybe just for something new to do! But that's it! Buddhu, Sheikhu, both of you go home. I have to return all this, first to poor Sita Ram's family and then to that rascal Bhiku Ram. Wouldn't it be funny if I was caught now and hauled off to jail?' Grinning at the thought, Veeru walked off at a brisk pace.

Sheikh's admiration for Veeru grew. Only Veeru Bhaiyya could be so brave, so daring and so unselfish! Robber and saviour – all in one!

The following morning Sheikh was buying a new kite in the bazaar when someone nudged him. It was Veeru, looking smart and fresh, his eyes sparkling. Sheikh looked at him anxiously.

'Don't worry, champion! All is well!' Veeru clapped him on the shoulder. 'Meet me here this afternoon at four. I may have some news for you.'

Sheikh could hardly wait. Exactly at four o'clock Veeru and Buddhu appeared, marching smartly. 'Sheikhu my friend, this is goodbye,' said Veeru. 'Buddhu and I are off to join the army.' He saluted Sheikh with a flourish. So did Buddhu, smiling widely. 'Let's see what the world is like outside this village. Now you be a good boy, look after your mother and stay out of mischief. Stay away from dholaks and tandoors. Understand?'

Veeru was smiling. Sheikh smiled back, a sudden lump in his throat. He could imagine Veeru in his army uniform, looking as smart and splendid as a king! He would miss him. He would miss both Veeru Bhaiyya and Buddhu and the midnight adventures he had shared with them.

But then, Sheikh consoled himself, his small loss was going to be the army's big gain!

The Nightmare

Sheikh Chilli was being tormented by a recurring nightmare. He dreamt he was a mouse and all the cats of the village were chasing him. Night after tiresome night, Sheikh Chilli scurried between houses and inside houses, over furniture and under furniture and along village streets, trying to get away from the cats. Even after he woke up in the morning, he still imagined he was a mouse!

'Beta Sheikh, did you dream that dream again?' Sheikh Chilli's worried mother asked him one morning. 'You were uneasy and restless most of the night.'

Sheikh Chilli nodded, putting his arms around his mother and holding her tight. She was the only family he had.

'I'll take you to Hakimji today,' said his ammi. 'Inshallah, he'll put an end to your nightmares.'

The hakim listened patiently as Sheikh Chilli told him about the recurring nightmare.

'Why is my child suffering like this?' Sheikh's mother asked the hakim. 'When he was a baby, a wild cat scratched him badly, before I could save him. Could he be dreaming of that?'

'Perhaps,' said the hakim. 'But don't worry. These bad dreams will stop soon. Sheikh, come to me every evening for a few days for some medicine. And remember, you are not a mouse, you are a handsome young man.'

Sheikh smiled all over his good-natured face. Every evening the wise hakim spent almost an hour talking to the fatherless boy, before sending him home with some harmless medicine that ensured a good night's rest. And with the added reassurance that Sheikh was indeed a man and not a mouse!

Sheikh Chilli and the hakim became good friends. The hakim tried to teach him simple facts about health and hygiene.

'Beta Sheikh,' he said one evening, 'what would happen if one of my ears fell off?'

'Hakimji, you would become half-deaf,' said Sheikh, staring hard at the hakim's large ears.

'Quite right,' said the hakim. 'And if my other ear fell off too?'

'Then you would become blind, Hakimji,' said Sheikh.

'Blind?' asked the startled hakim.

'Yes,' said Sheikh. 'If you don't have ears, won't your spectacles fall off?'

The hakim burst out laughing. 'You are right, Sheikh beta', he said. 'I never thought of that!'

Gradually Sheikh's nightmares ceased. He stopped dreaming or imagining that he was a mouse. One evening an old friend of the hakim's came to see him. Sheikh was asked to go and buy hot jalebis from the bazaar. He was just stepping out when he saw a big cat a few feet away.

Sheikh let out a loud shriek and hid behind the hakim. 'Save me Hakimji!' squeaked Sheikh, trembling with fear.

'Dear child, you are no longer a mouse, don't you know that?'

'I know it Hakimji.' Sheikh was still scared. 'But has anyone told the cat?'

Hiding a smile, the hakim shooed the cat away,

and reassured Sheikh, before sending him off to get the jalebis.

'I knew this boy's father well,' declared the hakim's visitor, after he had been told a little bit about Sheikh Chilli. 'I would like to visit his house and pay my respects to his mother.'

'Sheikh will accompany you,' said the hakim.

After eating the crunchy jalebis and drinking some kehwa, Sheikh and the visitor left for Sheikh's house.

'So this road goes straight to your house, does it?'

'It doesn't,' said Sheikh.

The visitor was surprised. 'I thought it did,' he said.

'It doesn't,' said Sheikh.

'Then where does it go?' asked the visitor.

'It doesn't go anywhere,' said Sheikh calmly.

The visitor gaped at him. 'Beta, what do you mean?'

'Sir,' said Sheikh patiently. 'How can the road go anywhere? It has no legs. It is lifeless. It just lies where it is. But we can go on this road to my house. Ammi and I will be honoured to have you as our guest.'

The elderly man was touched by Sheikh's innocence. A few years later Sheikh Chilli became his son-in-law!

The Horse's Egg

Sheikh Chilli was flying a kite and dreaming of horses. Swift white stallions with flowing manes. 'Faster!' he urged his imaginary horse, tugging fiercely at the kite string. 'It's a matter of life and death! The princess needs me.'

'Before that, your mother needs you,' said his ammi, toiling up the stairs to the roof. 'Beta, how many times do I have to call you? Now stop flying your kite and go to the market.' She told him what to buy. 'And don't forget to ask the Lala for another job. You've been idling at home for two months.'

'Ammi,' said Sheikh as he went out of the house, 'wouldn't you like to have a horse? I could ride it to the market and you could sit behind me.'

His mother's tired face broke into a smile. 'Your two legs are enough for me', she said. 'I don't need four. Now do what I've told you to do and hurry back.'

Sheikh Chilli set off on foot but in his mind he was galloping down the road on a beautiful white horse! *Dhuk! Dhurruk! Dhuk! Dhurruk!*

'Hey! Watch where you're going!' said Lalian. He had been adjusting the chain on his bicycle and Sheikh Chilli had almost banged into him!

'Sorry Lallan,' said Sheikh amiably. 'Is this your new cycle?'

'Brand-new!' boasted Lallan. 'I bought it yesterday.'

'What I want to buy is a horse,' Sheikh said earnestly. 'A white horse that runs like the wind! But I don't have much money.'

Lallan's eyes gleamed. Here was another chance to make a fool of Sheikh. 'How much do you have?' he asked casually.

'Five rupees,' said Sheikh promptly. 'And I'll have some more when I start earning again.'

'Hmm!' Lallan pretended to think. 'A friend of

mine deals in horses. He might sell you one for five rupees to begin with. Let me find out. Meet me here after two hours.'

Sheikh nodded happily. Feeling very excited he rushed to the market, bought what his mother wanted and rushed home. In two hours he was back at the spot where he had met Lallan, with five rupees in his pocket. Lallan was waiting for him, holding a large watermelon. Sheikh Chilli was taken aback though watermelons were his favourite fruit.

'I know what you're thinking,' said Lallan. 'But this is not a watermelon, though it looks like one. It's a horse's egg!'

'Really?' Sheikh Chilli was astonished. He had never heard of a horse's egg.

'My friend couldn't sell you a horse for five rupees,' said Lallan. 'But because I asked him to, he's willing to sell you this horse's egg. Take very good care of it. Cover it and keep it warm in a safe place at home. It will hatch soon and then you will be the owner of a beautiful white baby horse!'

Sheikh's eyes shone at the thought. In a daze of delight he handed Lallan five rupees and took the watermelon from him. 'Be careful you don't drop it!' said Lallan and watched with a wicked grin as Sheikh Chilli turned to go home, clutching his precious burden. He plodded along in the heat for several minutes, sweat dripping down his face and stinging his eyes. The horse's egg seemed to grow heavier with every step.

Sheikh Chilli decided to rest for a moment by the side of the road. But, as he was doing so, the watermelon slipped through his sweaty fingers, rolled on the grass, hit a tree and burst open!

Startled by the noise a white rabbit ran out of the bushes behind the tree and fled in the direction from which Sheikh had come. 'Oh no!' He was horrified. His baby horse was running away! He raced after it as fast as he could. The rabbit bounded through the grass with Sheikh Chilli in hot pursuit. And then, right in his path, taking a short cut home, was Lallan on his brand-new bicycle!

This time Sheikh banged into him good and proper. The bicycle went flying and Lallan landed on the ground with Sheikh on top of him. A couple of passers-by stopped to help. One of them was the hakim.

'Hakimji!' cried Sheikh Chilli. 'My baby horse is running away! Please stop him!'

'Don't worry Sheikh,' said the hakim calmly. 'We'll catch him.' He wondered what Sheikh was talking about as he helped the two boys to their feet. Sheikh Chilli was hardly injured. It was Lallan who was groaning, both in pain and at the sight of his new bicycle, now scratched and dented, its handle twisted and its left pedal broken. The rabbit had disappeared.

Hakimji escorted the groaning Lallan home. Sheikh Chilli accompanied them, wheeling the bicycle and relating the story of the horse's egg.

'Where will I find my horse now, Hakimji?' he asked anxiously, when the two of them were on their way to Sheikh's home. 'He ran away so fast, the little fellow!'

'Forget about him, Sheikhu,' said the hakim gently. 'You have got your five rupees back and Lallan has got what he deserves! Horses don't come out of eggs. Will you remember that?'

'Yes Hakimji,' said Sheikh Chilli obediently. 'But this one did,' he silently added. 'And I'll never forget the sight!'

The Kazi 1

Sheikh Chilli was an inveterate dreamer and an innocent fool to boot! This combination ensured that while getting a job was difficult for him, keeping one, once he got it, was even more difficult. Sheikh's mother was worried. If her son remained jobless, he was likely to remain unmarried as well.

'Son, you must find some work,' Sheikh Chilli's mother said anxiously, as she served him food one evening. 'You are a young man now. Soon it will be time to find a bride for you! But who will give his daughter to a man, who doesn't earn? Find yourself a good, steady job. I'm getting old. How long will I earn for the two of us?'

'Not long Ammi,' Sheikh said affectionately. 'Wait and see, I'll have a job by tomorrow evening.'

'May it be so, my son!' his ammi said fervently.

Getting a job was easier said than done! Whom should he approach, Sheikh wondered. Several people in the village had employed him. But no job had lasted more than a few weeks. The following morning he decided to ask Lala Teli Ram, the merchant, if he needed another helper.

'He might have forgotten the time I slipped and fell into the pond, while carrying a sack of salt for him,' thought Sheikh hopefully. Where did all that salt go? Deep in thought, he almost banged into two brothers who had been his classmates during the few months he had attended the village school some years ago.

'Mian, still daydreaming?' asked the older brother. 'No wonder Maulvi Sahib threw you out of school!'

'I was thinking of finding a job,' said Sheikh. 'Ammi says no one will marry me if I don't have a job.'

The two brothers started laughing. 'She is right,' said one of them, 'and we can suggest a job for you

43

straightaway, but it won't be easy. You'll be working for a cunning and stingy kazi. He'll offer you a salary of twenty rupees a month, free food and a place to stay. But then he will make your life so miserable that you'll quit the job very fast. When you do so, you'll forfeit that month's salary and in addition he'll snip off a piece of your ear! Many boys have worked for him. Like us, they have all had their ears snipped off. The last boy came back crying two days ago.'

'Suppose he turns his servant out, instead of the servant quitting?' asked Sheikh, thinking of the many masters who had dismissed him. 'Then will he have his own ear snipped off?'

'That hasn't happened yet and it is not likely to happen. Be careful Mian, Kazi Sahib is a very clever man!'

'Give me his address,' said Sheikh Chilli. 'I promised Ammi I would find a job by this evening.'

*

Sheikh walked several miles to the town where the kazi lived. He had just returned from court.

'Salaam Sarkar,' said Sheikh, 'I have come to work for you.'

The kazi looked at Sheikh's innocent face. Another bakra! he thought. He won't last long! Aloud he said,

44

'Do you know the conditions of employment?'

Sheikh nodded. 'Ji Sarkar! Twenty rupees a month, along with free food and a place to sleep.'

'In return for which, you will do whatever work is given to you,' said the kazi sternly. 'I will not turn you out. But if you quit the job, you will lose that month's salary and I will snip off a bit of your ear as a lifelong reminder to you of your slackness! Is that clear? Any questions?'

'Just one, Sarkar,' said Sheikh. 'If you turn me out—'

'That won't happen!' snapped the kazi.

'Ji Sarkar. But if it does, I'll take one year's salary and snip off a bit of your ear!'

The kazi's mouth fell open! No one had ever dared to say something so preposterous to him. This boy must be a real idiot!

'Very well,' he said coldly. 'I accept your conditions. Now go inside. Begum Sahiba will explain your duties to you.'

Sheikh's duties consisted of doing practically everything—sweeping and cleaning the house, washing the clothes, scrubbing the utensils, going to the market and looking after the kazi's three-year-old son. Sheikh obeyed every command with a smile and performed every task at his usual dreamy pace. As a result, no job was completed. He left the clothes half-washed when the kazi's wife called him to scrub utensils. He left half the utensils dirty because it was time to go to the market!

*

'What a fool you've found this time!' grumbled the kazi's wife. 'There isn't a single job he does properly.'

'He'll learn,' said the kazi. 'Or he'll quit. Be a little patient and make him work hard.'

Every night Sheikh fell into bed exhausted. One night the kazi roused him just as he was dreaming that he was decked up as a bridegroom!

'The child needs to relieve himself,' said the kazi. 'Take him outside and let him squat over the drain behind the house.'

Sheikh was rather annoyed to have his beautiful dream interrupted, but he got up and took the kazi's son outside. It was a dark, windy night and the child clung to Sheikh.

'Have you ever seen a ghost?' Sheikh asked the boy. The child clung even harder! 'Don't be scared,' said Sheikh. 'I can see something swimming in the drain. But it can't be a ghost. Ghosts don't know how to swim.'

The child burst into tears and ran back into the house, to his mother. Sheikh returned to dreaming of himself as a bridegroom while the kazi's son wet his mother's bed!

The begum was furious. 'Get rid of this idiot Sheikh Chilli!' she said to her husband early the following morning. 'He can't do a simple thing like taking the child out at night.'

'I can't get rid of him,' said the kazi grimly. 'But I'll teach him a lesson he won't forget.' He called Sheikh Chilli and said, 'I have ten bighas of land, near the jungle, just outside this town. Go there now. My bullocks and plough are with my neighbour, Ram Singh. Take them and plough the entire ten bighas. Do a good job. I'll check what you've done tomorrow. And before you come home, there are two more jobs for you. Catch a plump rabbit. I want some fine meat for dinner tonight. And don't forget to bring home a big load of firewood. Be here in the evening by the time I get back from court. Now go!'

'I've given the fool nothing to eat or drink this morning,' said the kazi's begum. 'Let him sweat on an empty stomach!'

'You can throw him a few bones to chew tonight!' said the kazi with a nasty laugh. 'That is if he doesn't run away after so much hard labour!'

Sheikh Chilli bought channa with the few coins he had in his pocket, drank some water and walked to the kazi's land. He yoked the bullocks to the plough and ambled through the kazi's fields with them till the sun was high in the sky. Suddenly, remembering his other two jobs, he looked around for firewood. All the trees he could have cut down, if he had the time, were too big or too far away. Then his eyes fell on the plough. Borrowing an axe from the astonished Ram Singh, Sheikh freed the bullocks and chopped up the plough!

Now all he had to do was catch a plump rabbit for the kazi's dinner. Sheikh had not seen a single mouse, leave alone a rabbit in the fields. But he had seen a dead dog lying on the road!

He returned to the kazi's house carrying the chopped-up plough on his head and dragging the dead dog by its tail.

'Sarkar,' he said cheerfully. 'This dog is bigger than any rabbit. It will make a fine meal for you! And I've brought plenty of firewood for which the plough came in very handy!'

'You idiot!' spluttered the kazi, his face purple with rage. 'Get out of my sight! I'll deal with you later.'

The Kazi 2

With every passing day, the kazi's begum was getting more exasperated with Sheikh Chilli and his foolish behaviour. 'Why don't you get rid of this fellow?' she asked the kazi irritably one night.

'And get my ear snipped off, pay this rascal one year's salary and become the laughing stock of the town? I won't do that,' the kazi replied.

'Then get me another servant,' fumed his wife. 'And keep your precious Sheikh Chilli for your own work.'

'Very well,' said the kazi. 'You give Sheikh Chilli as little food as possible, just short of starving him. I'll take him with me to court every day. Let's see how long he lasts, with no work and no food.'

But the kazi was mistaken. Sheikh was quite happy sitting outside the court daydreaming or chatting with the other workers. When they heard how little he got to eat, they willingly shared their food with him!

One morning the kazi's wife sent her new servant to court with a message for the kazi. She needed money to buy some flour. The gatekeeper did not allow the servant to enter the courtroom.

'I'll help you,' said Sheikh. He stood in the doorway and yelled, 'Sarkar, there is no money in the house and no flour! Do something quickly!'

The kazi was most embarrassed. 'Idiot!' he rebuked Sheikh later. 'Don't you dare disturb me in the courtroom again!'

A few days later, a fire broke out in the kazi's house. The begum's new servant came running to inform the kazi. 'You go back home and help,' Sheikh told him. 'I'll inform Kazi Sahib.' Since he had been ordered not to disturb the kazi in the courtroom, he waited patiently till the evening. By then more than half the kazi's house had burnt down!

*

The kazi's begum came from a rich business family. The kazi decided to visit his in-laws to ask for a loan to rebuild the burnt portion of his house. He took Sheikh Chilli with him on horseback to keep him out of mischief.

The kazi's in-laws lived more than fifty miles away. On the way, the kazi, who had a slightly upset stomach, went into the jungle to relieve himself. Sheikh Chilli stood patiently beside the kazi's horse. A passing party of travellers thought Sheikh Chilli was the owner of the horse.

'We'll give you two hundred rupees for this horse,' they said to him. 'Will you sell it?'

'Yes,' said Sheikh. He took the money, snipped off a bit of the horse's tail and stuck the hairs into a hole in the ground.

'Hurry Sarkar, hurry!' he yelled as soon as he saw the kazi approaching. 'The horse is being dragged into a mouse hole! If you help me, we can pull him out!' The bewildered kazi held on to Sheikh. Sheikh tugged at the horsehairs stuck in the hole. Out they came and both Sheikh and the kazi fell in a heap!

'The mice were too strong for us, Sarkar,' Sheikh said sadly. 'The horse has gone right in. Now we'll need powerful men with shovels to dig him out!'

'What rubbish you are talking, you fool!' snapped the kazi. 'How can a horse disappear into a mouse hole? You rogue! What have you done with him? Lost him or sold him? And how do we travel now? On foot?'

'Sarkar, there is a village close by where you can get a new horse,' said Sheikh. 'What is the loss of one horse for a great man like yourself?'

Grumbling, the kazi bought another horse at the next village and did not let it out of sight for a second! He rode the horse himself and made Sheikh walk, as punishment for losing the first horse.

They stopped for the night at a sarai. The kazi had his meal, threw a few rotis at Sheikh and said, 'Stay with the horse all night. Keep massaging him and don't dare let him out of your sight! Do you hear me?'

'Ji Sarkar,' said Sheikh meekly, hiding a yawn. Exhausted after his long walk, he settled himself beside the horse and began wearily to massage him. Sheikh did not know when he fell asleep and when someone quietly took the horse away! He awoke in the morning and found the horse missing. Sheikh looked around desperately. The kazi would skin him alive if he didn't find the horse fast! Then he saw two long ears half-hidden in the grass the horse had been eating.

'Aha!' said Sheikh grabbing the ears, 'so that's where you've hidden yourself!'

The ears belonged to a rabbit. Sheikh was staring at it when the kazi appeared.

'Where's the horse?' he demanded.

'Here it is, Sarkar,' said Sheikh promptly.

'Idiot! That is a rabbit, not a horse!'

'Sarkar, it's really a horse. I massaged it so much that it became the size of a rabbit. I didn't massage the ears. Look! They are still the same size!'

'You are the world's biggest fool!' said the kazi, his voice trembling with anger. 'And I am the second biggest fool for having employed you! Now get ready, it's time to leave.'

They walked the rest of the way to their destination where they received a warm welcome.

*

The kazi's mother-in-law took Sheikh Chilli aside. 'Your master doesn't look too well,' she said. 'I hope it is nothing more than the fatigue of the journey.'

'His stomach has been a little upset,' said Sheikh.

'In that case, I'll cook him some khichri,' said the old lady.

'But make it spicy!' said Sheikh. 'He loves spicy food.'

At dinnertime Sheikh Chilli was served the most delicious biryani, mutton curry, vegetables and kheer.

All that the kazi was served was a large bowl of spicy khichri!

The kazi was so hungry that he ate it all. He woke up in the middle of the night with a stomach-ache and an urgent need to relieve himself.

'I have to go outside,' he shook Sheikh awake. 'Come with me.'

'Sarkar,' said Sheikh sleepily, 'there is an earthen pot lying in the corner. Why not use that? It can be emptied in the morning.'

The kazi had to relieve himself several times during the course of the night. By morning the pot was half-full.

'Go and throw it out,' he ordered Sheikh Chilli.

'I can't, Sarkar,' said Sheikh. 'I'm not a scavenger.'

The kazi was in a fix. Angrily, he picked up the pot himself and went out to throw it in the jungle. His brother-in-law came running after him. The embarrassed kazi increased his pace. But his brother-in-law caught up with him.

'Bhaijan, where are you going with that load on your head? Let me help you with it,' he said.

'No! No!' protested the kazi. 'It is all right.' He tried to retain his hold on the pot. But it slipped from his hands, fell between the two men and splattered them both with its foul contents!

Sheikh had been watching from the window.

'Sarkar,' he cried, running up to the kazi. 'I hope you are not hurt!'

The kazi folded his hands in entreaty. 'I beg you Sheikh Chilli, leave me alone,' he said. 'I've had enough of you! You win. And I lose. You are hereby dismissed. Take an entire year's salary; cut both my ears off! But never let me set eyes on you again!'

'You can keep your ears, Sarkar,' said Sheikh. 'And here are the two hundred rupees I got for selling your first horse. I'm sorry the second one turned into a rabbit! You shouldn't have told me to massage him all night!'

With one year's salary in his pocket, Sheikh Chilli returned home to a hero's welcome!

Half of That

Sheikh Chilli was lying on the ground and groaning loudly. His mother hurried into the room. 'Beta, what happened? How did you hurt yourself?'

Still groaning, Sheikh got up onto his bed and rolled till he fell off it for the second time. 'Like this!' he said. 'I hurt myself like this! Hai! Ammi, I'm dying!'

'You are not dying, you stupid boy!' his mother said sharply, as she helped him to his feet. 'Who told you to fall off your bed again? I asked you to tell me, not to show me, how you got hurt.'

'You didn't,' protested Sheikh. 'You just said—how did you hurt yourself? You didn't say—just tell me, don't show me. I showed you because *showing* you was a better way than *telling* you. And now when I'm in such pain, you're getting angry with me!'

'I'm not getting angry,' said his mother in exasperation. 'Really! Sheikh, it's impossible to reason with you! Now lie quietly while I rub some balm on your back.'

By the following morning Sheikh Chilli was feeling much better. 'I am going out for a while,' he said to his mother.

'Why not go to the market and buy yourself a new pair of chappals?' she suggested. 'You need them.'

'I'll go to the new shoe shop!' Sheikh said excitedly.

'Then be careful,' said his ammi. 'I've heard that shopkeeper is a bit of a crook. Pay him only half of what he asks for.'

'I'll remember that,' said Sheikh. 'Don't worry.'

The new shoe shop was bigger and fancier than the old one. Sheikh was the first customer of the day and the shopkeeper was anxious to make a sale. He showed Sheikh Chilli many chappals of different designs and colours, and Sheikh tried on all of them.

Finally he pointed to a plain blue and white pair and asked, 'How much are these?'

'Just eight rupees,' said the shopkeeper.

Sheikh remembered his mother's words. 'Pay half of what he asks for,' she had said.

'I'll give you four rupees for them,' said Sheikh. 'Take it or leave it.'

'Four rupees?' protested the shopkeeper. 'You must be joking, huzoor! But it is your first visit to my shop and you are my first customer today, so as a very special favour, I'll let you have the chappals for four rupees.'

'Then I'll take them for two rupees,' said Sheikh.

The shopkeeper's mouth fell open in amazement. He glared at Sheikh. 'I was selling you the chappals at half the price as a special favour for a new customer. But you are trying to cheat me! All right. Take the chappals for two rupees and go! And don't come back!'

But Sheikh still hadn't forgotten his mother's words, 'Pay half', she had said.

'Then I'll take them for one rupee!' he said brightly.

The shopkeeper's face turned red with rage. 'Take them for nothing!' he hissed, thrusting the chappals at Sheikh Chilli. 'They're yours! Take them for nothing and get out of my shop!'

What was half of nothing, Sheikh wondered as he left the market behind him. Whatever it was, his ammi would be happy he had followed her instructions. And how beautiful she looked when she was happy!

Admiring the smart new blue and white chappals now on his feet, Sheikh Chilli walked home.

In the City

Sheikh Chilli had been leading a comfortable life, for the past few months—flying kites, lazing around, playing the fool and of course, dreaming. But, one day Sheikh discovered to his dismay that the money he had earned from the kazi was fast running out. So he reluctantly set off to the nearest town in search of another job. On the road, ahead of him, was a stout man, walking slowly, with a large tin on his head. He was sweating profusely.

'Listen,' he said as Sheikh passed him, 'I'll give

you two annas if you'll carry this tin of ghee till we reach the city.'

Happy to earn some money, Sheikh placed the tin on his own head and continued walking. But as he walked, he began to dream. With these two annas I'll buy some chicks, he thought. When the chicks grow up, I'll have lots of hens and lots of eggs. I'll sell the eggs and make a fortune! Then I'll buy the biggest house in the village and marry the most beautiful girl in the world! Ammi will never need to work again. She and my begum will sit like queens, surrounded by forty servants! I'll fly kites the whole day long— huge, multicoloured kites made especially for me. The entire village will come to watch me flying my kites—Phrrr! Phrrr!

Sheikh flung his hands about, flying imaginary kites. The tin of ghee fell off his head and crashed to the ground, spilling all the ghee!

'Idiot! What have you done?' yelled the stout man. 'You've spilt thirty rupees worth of pure ghee!'

'What is thirty rupees compared to an entire fortune?' said Sheikh sadly. 'That is what I've lost!'

The stout man stomped off in a temper while Sheikh walked on till he reached the gate of a large house, outside which stood a horse-drawn carriage.

'Kochvanji,' Sheikh addressed the driver of the carriage, 'do you know where I can get a job? I'm willing to do anything.'

'You could try inside, I think the cook is looking for a helper,' suggested the driver.

Sheikh went round to the back of the house, met the cook and got the job. He worked hard the rest of the day, cutting vegetables and scrubbing utensils. By nightfall, he was both exhausted and famished.

'Here!' said the cook, throwing him two stale rotis smeared with pickle. 'You can sleep outside my room but be sure to wake up at the crack of dawn. Work in this house starts early.'

Sheikh fell fast asleep the moment he lay down. He woke up in the middle of the night, feeling very hungry. He tried hard to go back to sleep, but hunger pangs kept him awake. Finally he got up and peeped into the cook's room. It was empty but he could hear voices in the garden outside. Sheikh went closer. The cook and the gardener were talking quietly. On the ground, between them, was a big pile of lemons.

'This time I've found a good buyer,' Sheikh heard the gardener say. 'He will pay us almost double of what we have been getting so far!'

'Good!' said the cook. 'The old lady doesn't suspect a thing!'

Sheikh cleared his throat to attract their attention. The two thieves got a jolt when they saw him!

'I'm very hungry,' said Sheikh. 'I couldn't sleep.'

The cook was in a fix. He didn't know whether Sheikh wanted food or money to keep his mouth shut about what he had just overheard. He took some coins out of his pocket and thrust them at Sheikh. 'Not a word to anyone!' he snarled. 'Now go!'

'I'm going,' said Sheikh. But where was he to go to buy food for himself in the middle of the night? He went towards the gate, stumbling over the sleeping driver as he did so and waking him up. When the driver asked Sheikh Chilli where he was going at that late hour, Sheikh told him the whole story.

'Oho! So that's what the two of them are up to!' said the driver. 'I had my suspicions. The first thing I'm going to do in the morning is to tell Bibiji that she's been housing two thieves! I'll see that they are both thrown out!'

They were! And Sheikh received a reward of fifty rupees for having caught them. A new cook and a new gardener were employed. Sheikh was promoted from being the cook's helper to being the driver's assistant. In a short while, he learnt to drive the carriage and when the driver went on leave, Sheikh drove Bibiji wherever she wanted to go.

But then Bibiji's son and daughter-in-law came to live with her and Sheikh Chilli was in trouble again!

'Sit up straight!' the young man ordered him. 'Drive smartly and keep your mouth shut at all times.

I don't like sloppy, talkative drivers.'

'Ji Sarkar!' said Sheikh and tried to do exactly as he was told.

One evening he drove the young couple to the market. The lady dropped her purse by mistake when she was getting into the carriage to come home. Sheikh saw this but said nothing since he had been told to keep his mouth shut at all times.

'You fool!' shouted his master when he learnt that Sheikh had seen the purse drop. 'In future pick up anything you see drop. Understand?'

'Ji, Sarkar!' said Sheikh.

A few days later, his master was entertaining some guests when Sheikh entered the room with a packet in his hands.

'Sarkar, this had dropped on the road,' he said, placing the packet on a table. 'I picked it up as you had told me to do.'

'What's in it?' asked one of the guests. Sheikh obligingly opened the packet. It was full of dung that the horse had dropped and Sheikh, obeying instructions, had carefully picked it all up!

'Out!' yelled his master, furious at being embarrassed in front of his guests. 'Leave my house this very instant. You are dismissed!'

Another job gone, thought Sheikh sadly, and for no fault of mine. But he brightened up when he remembered the four months' salary he had saved as well as the fifty rupees that Bibiji had given him.

Ammi will be pleased, he thought, as he began walking back to his village. With this money she'll be able to buy lots of chicks. The chicks will grow up and turn into hens ... Daydreaming happily, he continued on his way.

Visit to the In-laws

Sheikh Chilli's ammi could not contain her happiness.
The impossible had happened. A bride had been
found for her son! Fawzia was a beautiful, moon-
faced girl. Fawzia's father had known Sheikh's father,
and had taken a liking to Sheikh when he had met
him some years ago, at the house of the hakim. Sheikh
and Fawzia were soon married.

A few months after his marriage, Sheikh Chilli
was invited to visit the home of his in-laws. He set
off early in the morning, dressed in his best clothes

and was warmly received by his wife's parents, brother and sisters.

After he had eaten a hearty meal, his brother-in-law offered Sheikh a paan. Sheikh had never eaten a paan before. Nevertheless, he popped it into his mouth and started chewing. As he did so, he happened to see his face in a mirror hanging on the wall. A thin stream of red betel juice was trickling from his mouth to his chin. Sheikh mistook it for blood. He was terrified!

I'm dying! he thought. Something has suddenly broken inside me or maybe they've poisoned me! Whatever it is, I'm dying.

His eyes filled with tears. Without saying a word he got up, went to his room and lay down on the bed. Wondering what had upset him, his brother-in-law followed Sheikh. Seeing him lying there weeping and refusing to say a word, he didn't know what to do! Just then Sheikh's father-in-law entered the room.

'Beta, tell me what is wrong,' he said to Sheikh gently. 'Are you in pain?'

'Abbu, I am dying!' declared Sheikh. 'My blood is flowing out of me.' He pointed to his red, paan-stained lips with a shaking finger.

'Is that all?' asked his father-in-law, suppressing a smile.

'What more do you want, Abbu?' Sheikh was

rather annoyed.

Sheikh Chilli's Abbu then gently told him the difference between betel juice and blood. The mystery of his sudden illness was solved! A relieved Sheikh bounced out of bed and went for a long walk with his brother-in-law to see the sights of the town.

It was dark by the time they returned. Sheikh went to bed and fell fast asleep. He was woken up later in the night by the drone of a mosquito. Sheikh tried unsuccessfully to slap it away. Finally he hurled his chappal at it in the dark. The mosquito stopped droning and Sheikh went back to sleep. But his chappal had hit a small pot full of honey, suspended from a wooden beam above his head. The pot tilted and honey began dripping on to his face. In his dream, Sheikh began to enjoy the honey's sweetness. But when he woke before dawn, he found his entire body soaked in honey!

He had to get to the stream nearby to wash it off. Next to his room was a store from where he could leave the house without waking up anyone. Sheikh tiptoed into the store and walked straight into a huge pile of cotton wool lying ready to be made into quilts for the winter.

The cotton wool stuck to his sticky hair, face and body. He was groping in the dark for the back door when one of his sisters-in-law came into the store to get something. Seeing a strange furry figure she screamed, 'Ghost! Ghost!' and ran from the room.

Sheikh found the back door and fled from the house towards the stream. It was further away than he had thought. On the way was a sheep pen. Sheikh sat down among the sheep to rest for a few minutes. The warmth of their bodies had almost lulled him to sleep when he realised that someone was moving stealthily among the animals. It was a thief! Before Sheikh could react, the thief had thrown a blanket over him, hoisted Sheikh on to his back and started running!

'Arrey! What are you doing?' said Sheikh indignantly, struggling to free himself. 'I'm not a sheep!'

A talking animal! The thief got a fright! He dropped both Sheikh and the blanket and took to his heels.

Sheikh jumped into the stream and scrubbed away all the cotton wool and honey. Covering himself with the blanket that the thief had dropped, he walked back home.

'Bhaijan, where have you been?' asked his brother-in-law. 'Thank God you are safe! There is a ghost in the room next to yours! We are just going to fetch someone to tackle it.'

'No need,' said Sheikh Chilli calmly. 'I can tackle

the ghost.'

Sheikh Chilli then shut himself up in the store, whacked the pile of cotton wool several times with a broom and loudly uttered a spell he had just made up! Then he emerged from the room victorious, and spent the rest of his visit basking in the admiration of the entire family and neighbourhood!

The Guest Who Would Not Leave

Sheikh Chilli was a disaster at keeping house. The last time he had been left alone he had almost set the house on fire! No wonder then that Sheikh's mother and wife were extremely worried. They were going to be away for a month and the prospect of leaving Sheikh Chilli alone in the house was making them very nervous.

Recalling the disaster, Fawzia said apprehensively to Sheikh Chilli, 'If we leave you here alone for a month, only Allah knows what might happen!'

'Begum, you worry unnecessarily,' Sheikh assured her. 'I am perfectly capable of looking after myself as well as the house. But to set your mind at rest, let me tell you that in your absence, I intend to visit my old friend and cousin Irfan Bhai.'

'Good!' said his relieved wife. 'Please come back a day after our return.'

Sheikh Chilli's cousin Irfan lived in a nearby village with his wife and two children. He owned a small shop that sold cloth. Irfan had spent many days of his youth with Sheikh and his mother. They had always looked after him, though there had been days when Sheikh's ammi had not known where their next meal was coming from!

Now, many years later when Sheikh appeared unexpectedly at his door, Irfan was very pleased. Here was a chance to repay some of that hospitality.

The first week of Sheikh's stay passed very pleasantly. However, when he showed no signs of leaving, Irfan's wife began to fret and fume.

'How long is your cousin going to stay?' she asked her husband.

'As long as he likes,' replied Irfan. 'Why should you be bothered? He spends the whole day with me in the shop and helps you with the children every evening.'

'That may be so,' said his wife grumpily, 'but see how much he eats! Look at the extra expense!'

'I owe his family too much to worry about a little expense,' said Irfan. 'And if you, my dear Begum, ate a little less yourself, feeding one guest for a few days wouldn't be such a serious matter!'

His plump wife shed angry tears. 'It's no use talking to you,' she sniffed. 'I'll have to think of something.'

*

A few days later, when Irfan returned home with Sheikh, he found his wife and children ready for a journey.

'Bhaijan,' Irfan's wife said to Sheikh, 'I have received news that my father is very unwell. We will be leaving for my father's house this very night.'

'May Allah protect your father, Bhabiji,' said Sheikh. 'Please go with a carefree mind. I will look after this house till your return.'

'B-but Bhaijan,' protested Irfan's wife, 'how will you stay here? There is nothing to eat in the house. You would be better off returning home.'

'Then I'll leave tomorrow morning,' said Sheikh. 'My house is locked. Let me decide tonight which neighbour I should go to.'

The next morning, Sheikh decided to tidy the house a little before he left. As he rolled up the children's bedding, he found a key under the mattress. It was the key to the kitchen cupboard, hidden there by Irfan's wife! The cupboard contained enough atta and dal for several days.

Now I needn't go home before Ammi and Fawzia get back, thought Sheikh happily and proceeded to cook himself a meal.

Meanwhile, Irfan was furious when he discovered that his wife had concocted the entire story of her father's illness. The family returned home after two days to be warmly greeted by Sheikh Chilli!

Another few days went by. Sheikh still showed no signs of leaving. Irfan's wife was getting desperate. One evening, she took to her bed, groaning loudly.

'Hai!' she moaned to her husband, 'this pain will kill me! It's exactly like the pain Bhaijan said his ammi used to get. Ask him to go to the same hakim who cured his ammi and get some medicine prepared for me. He needn't come back all the way with the medicine. We can send someone for it. But ask Bhaijan to hurry up and go!'

'Bhabhiji, I'll leave as soon as it is daylight,' Sheikh assured her. 'I may lose my way in the dark. Inshallah, you will be well soon!'

Irfan's wife groaned throughout the night.

Hearing her groans in the next room Sheikh had a nightmare. He dreamt that a ferocious lion was pursuing him! Trying to get away from the lion, Sheikh fell off his bed and rolled right under it. The nightmare ended and he slept peacefully the rest of the night.

Early next morning, Irfan saw Sheikh's empty bed. 'Begum, he's already left,' Irfan called out to his wife.

She jumped out of bed and came running. 'I wasn't really ill!' she said with a laugh to her astonished husband.

'And I haven't really gone!' said Sheikh Chilli, emerging from under the bed. 'Just as well, since Bhabhiji is so much better!'

The Black Thread

Sheikh Chilli was again jobless! With no other means of earning money in sight, he decided to go to the forest and chop wood. It was a pleasant day and Sheikh set off cheerfully, swinging his axe.

On reaching the forest, Sheikh Chilli climbed a tree and started chopping down a sturdy branch. Several ants were crawling past him up the branch. Sheikh observed them closely. How busy they were! But where were they going? He turned around to watch them crawling up the trunk of the tree and continued chopping the branch, taking care to brush the ants away before he did so.

They must be going to meet their sultan, thought Sheikh. They will tell him about me. The sultan will come in person to meet me. There will be a tiny gold turban on his head. That is how I will recognise him! He will thank me for saving so many of his subjects. He will ask me what he can do for me. He will offer me ...

Suddenly a passer-by yelled, 'Watch out! You are going to fall!'

KRRRAACKKK! The branch Sheikh had been chopping came crashing down, with Sheikh on it!

'Are you hurt?' enquired the passer-by, helping Sheikh to his feet.

'No,' said Sheikh. Luckily he had fallen on a thick pile of leaves. 'Tell me, how did you know I was going to fall? Are you an astrologer?'

The passer-by was a tailor, not an astrologer! But seeing a chance to make some money, he nodded.

'Give me one rupee,' he said. 'I will tell you your entire future.'

'I have only one anna,' said Sheikh, fishing it out of his pocket and offering it. 'At least tell me how long I'm going to live.'

The tailor pretended to look closely at Sheikh's palm.

'Death is stalking you!' he said gravely.

'Hai Allah!' moaned Sheikh.

'But this will protect you,' said the tailor, taking some black thread out of his pocket, muttering something over it and tying it around Sheikh's neck. 'As long as this thread remains unbroken, you will remain alive!'

Sheikh thanked him, picked up the fallen branch and walked home, deep in thought.

'What is the matter?' asked Fawzia, putting down the embroidery she did to earn some money, and fetching him a glass of cool water to drink. Nervously fingering the black thread around his neck, Sheikh told her what had happened in the forest.

Fawzia burst out laughing. 'You are a real simpleton!' she said affectionately. 'Fancy believing whatever rubbish that man told you! All he wanted was the money in your pocket and you gave it to him!'

The next instant she grabbed the black thread, pulled it and broke it. 'Now you can forget all this nonsense!' she said.

Sheikh lay down at once and shut his eyes.

'What happened?' asked Fawzia.

'I'm dead,' said Sheikh. 'You broke the thread and I'm dead.'

His mother entered the house at that moment.

'Hai Allah!' she cried, 'what has happened to my child?'

'Ammiji, your precious son thinks he's dead!' said her daughter-in-law and narrated the whole story. Now it was his ammi's turn to marvel at Sheikh's foolishness! Nothing she or Fawzia said convinced Sheikh that he was still alive!

Giving up, the two women began attending to their household chores, while Sheikh lay stiffly on the ground. After a while, he opened his eyes and looked around, but shut them quickly when he saw his wife looking at him!

Fawzia was an intelligent woman. 'Ammiji,' she said loudly, 'this is a house of mourning now. Who can think of eating sweets at such a time? Let us throw away the hot gulab jamuns you have brought.'

Gulab jamuns? His favourite sweets! Sheikh forgot about being dead. 'No! No!' he said, sitting up. 'Don't throw them away. I've come back to life!'

The Courier

Sheikh Chilli's wife Fawzia had asked him to buy some things from the market. He was on his way when he saw the hakim walking briskly on the road ahead of him. Sheikh Chilli ran to catch up with the old man who had always helped and advised his ammi and him.

'Hakimji, where are you off to?' Sheikh asked affectionately.

'To see a patient, Sheikh,' replied the hakim.

'May I come with you?' asked Sheikh on a sudden

impulse, quite forgetting what he had set out to do.

'If you wish,' said the hakim with a smile.

Sheikh followed him when he entered the front room of a small house where a young boy of seven or eight lay, holding his stomach and groaning. The hakim examined his patient for a few moments. Then he turned to the boy's anxious mother.

'Don't worry,' he said. 'Your son will be fine. He has been eating too many raw guavas. That's all!' He handed the relieved woman some medicine, instructed her when to give it, and left. The entire visit had taken barely ten minutes.

Sheikh Chilli was most impressed. 'Hakimji,' he said eagerly, when they were on the road again, 'how did you know that the boy had been eating raw guavas?'

The hakim smiled. 'I know what little rascals of that age are normally up to!' he said. 'And didn't you see the seeds and pieces of guava skin under the bed?'

Once again Sheikh Chilli was right behind the hakim when he entered the house of his next patient. This time the patient was an elderly man who was obviously in great pain. As the hakim began to examine him, Sheikh glanced under the patient's bed. Just one rubber sandal was visible.

'Don't worry,' said Sheikh in a loud whisper to the patient's wife. 'Hakimji's medicine will soon cure your husband. But don't let him eat any more rubber sandals.'

'Sheikh!' The hakim's voice was stern though there was a glint of amusement in his eyes. 'You have work to do in the market, don't you? Go and do it.'

Obediently Sheikh Chilli left the house and walked the rest of the way to the market. He bought a kilo of mutton and was more than halfway home when he realised he had forgotten to buy the onions and spices for the meat. He stopped, put the mutton down for a moment and scratched his head, wondering what to do.

With lightning speed, an eagle swooped down on the meat and flew away with a piece in its beak, in the general direction of Sheikh's home.

'That's the answer!' he said with a grin. Leaving the rest of the meat on the ground, he watched from behind a tree. Down came the eagle again for another piece of the mutton.

'Take it all, piece by piece, to my wife!' Sheikh called out to the eagle as it flew away. 'Ours is the last house in the lane, right next to the fields. I'll get the onions and spices till then.'

He ran back to the market, bought what he had to and returned. Not a single piece of mutton was left on the ground.

'Good bird!' said Sheikh with great satisfaction.

He reached home and handed over the onions and spices to his wife.

'But where is the mutton?' she asked.

'Hasn't it reached?' Sheikh was surprised. He told Fawzia how he had instructed the eagle to deliver the meat to his doorstep.

Fawzia shook her head in disbelief. 'You actually told the eagle …?'

'Yes, I did,' said Sheikh proudly. 'Wasn't it a good idea?'

Fawzia didn't know whether to laugh or cry. There was no mutton for dinner that night. And the next time Fawzia wanted to buy some, she went to the market herself!

The Bottle of Oil

One morning Sheikh Chilli stormed into the local post office. Fawzia, who was visiting her parents, had not received the bottle of jasmine oil that Sheikh had sent her. There was no one in the post office at that hour except Somnath, the babu to whom Sheikh had entrusted the oil. Seeing Somnath, Sheikh Chilli demanded, 'Where is the bottle of jasmine oil I sent by post ten days ago? My wife's letter says she still hasn't received it.'

Somnath apologised. He was thinking hard. He

knew that he better come up with a quick excuse. If Sheikh Chilli was foolish enough to send an unpacked bottle of oil by post the way people sent money by money order, then he was foolish enough to believe anything! Somnath said with a straight face, 'When your bottle of oil was going out of this post office, someone's stick was coming in. The stick hit your bottle and broke it. I'm really very sorry.'

Sheikh's face fell. 'So that's what happened,' he said. 'When I catch the owner of that stick, I'll give him a good beating. With his own stick!'

'Yes, do that,' said Somnath, laughing inwardly.

Sheikh Chilli went home, feeling dejected. The oil was spilt, the money spent on it wasted. And Fawzia would not get her favourite hair oil that she had wanted to share with her mother. In his mind Sheikh saw the bottle of oil and the big stick rushing towards each other, followed by a crash! The bottle broke into bits and jasmine oil smeared the stick and everything else near it.

'Now everyone's letters will be covered with oil,' thought Sheikh Chilli angrily, 'all because of that stick! I have to find its owner and tick him off. The babu will know where he lives.'

Sheikh Chilli decided to go back to the post office that evening. But when he got there, it was shut. The two babus who worked there lived just behind it.

Sheikh went to Somnath's house and knocked on the front door. Munni, the babu's little daughter, opened it and smiled at Sheikh. They had often met at the kite seller's.

'My father will be home soon,' said the child and invited Sheikh into the house. He looked around as she went into the kitchen to fetch him a glass of water. Clothes hung from nails on the walls. Books and papers were scattered on a straw mat. A mirror stood on a wooden shelf in a corner of the room. Beside it lay a comb, a half-full bottle of oil and a new bottle just like the one he had sent his wife. He was staring at it when Munni came back into the room.

'Sheikh Chacha, do you like jasmine oil?' she asked shyly.

Sheikh nodded. When he told her what had happened to his bottle, she picked up the new one and handed it to him. 'Take it,' she said. 'We still have half a bottle.'

Sheikh smiled and patted her head. 'Munni, I can't take it,' he said. 'It's yours.'

The front door opened and both the babus from the post office walked in. Before Sheikh Chilli could say anything or replace the bottle on the shelf, Munni ran to her father and repeated the story she had just heard about the bottle and the stick.

'Papa,' she pleaded, 'let Sheikh Chacha have our

new bottle. His bottle broke and we still have our old one.'

'Munni is right,' said the older babu. He sounded both amused and firm. 'What do you say, Somnath?'

The guilty man knew the game was up! He could fool his daughter and Sheikh Chilli, but he couldn't fool his own colleague. 'Take the bottle,' he said to Sheikh.

'With our compliments,' added the older babu. 'The post office is sorry for what happened.'

Sheikh Chilli's smile lit up his entire face. He went home happily with his *own* bottle of oil! Though, of course he didn't know that.

The Leopard

Sheikh Chilli was looking dreamily in the mirror, twirling an imaginary moustache. After all, he was now a respected member of society. An employee of the Nawab of Jhajjar, no less. A moustache befitted a man of his stature, he thought. Fortune had finally smiled on him!

While he stood thus immersed in his dreams, he heard sounds in the courtyard. He rushed outside to find that the Nawab was setting out on a shooting expedition. Sheikh Chilli begged to be taken along.

The Nawab was amused. 'Arrey Mian, what will you do in the depths of the jungle?' he asked. 'It's no place to daydream! Have you ever killed a mouse that you are now ready to shoot a leopard?'

'Sarkar, I only need a chance to prove myself,' said Sheikh Chilli with great dignity.

So with rifle in hand, Sheikh Chilli accompanied the shooting party and soon found himself on a machan. Only a short distance away, tied to a tree, was a goat—live bait for the leopard. It was a moonlit night. The leopard would be clearly visible when it pounced on the terrified goat. The Nawab and his prize shooters waited silently on other machans for the leopard to appear.

An hour went by. Sheikh Chilli began to get restless. 'Where is the wretched leopard?' he whispered to the shooter who was with him on the machan.

'Be quiet!' hissed his companion. 'You'll ruin everything!'

Sheikh Chilli lapsed into an uncomfortable silence. What kind of hunt is this? he thought. We are all sitting, hidden in trees, waiting for one poor animal! We should be advancing on foot, with our rifles held ready! But they say the leopard runs very fast. He races through the jungle like my kite used to race across the sky!

Never mind. We'll run after him. We'll chase him relentlessly. Slowly the other shooters will be left behind. I'll outrun them. I'll close in on the leopard. He'll know I'm right behind him. He'll know his end is near. He'll stop. He'll turn. He'll look straight into my eyes. Into the eyes of his killer! Then I'll …

BANG! The leopard fell dead, a few inches away from the trembling goat on which it had been about to pounce!

One of the shooters went carefully towards the leopard to make sure that it was dead. It was. But who had shot it and so expertly?

Sheikh Chilli's companion thumped him hard on his back.

'That was fantastic!' he said. 'You surprised us all!'

'Shabash Mian! Shabash!' The Nawab congratulated Sheikh Chilli as the entire party gathered to inspect the leopard that Sheikh had shot. 'I thought no shooter could challenge me, but Sheikh Chilli has done it! That was a fine shot!'

Sheikh Chilli bowed his head modestly. He had absolutely no idea when the leopard had appeared and how his rifle had gone off, killing it in one shot!

But the leopard was dead. And he was a champion! That, at least, was beyond doubt!

Chhotey Nawab and the Liar

Sheikh Chilli was a little uneasy. The Nawab of Jhajjar
had gone to fight a battle. He was likely to be away
for several months. In his place, Chhotey Nawab, his
younger brother, was looking after state affairs.

While the Nawab had grown fond of Sheikh Chilli
and found his simplicity rather refreshing, Chhotey
Nawab considered Sheikh Chilli a fool and a shirker.

One day Chhotey Nawab upbraided Sheikh Chilli
in front of the entire court.

'A good worker does far more than the work

assigned to him, whereas you cannot do even a simple job correctly,' he said. 'You take a horse to the stable and forget to tie it up. You carry a load and either drop it or stumble over your own feet! Why don't you pay attention to what you are doing?'

Many of the courtiers tittered while Sheikh Chilli hung his head. A few days later, he was passing by Chhotey Nawab's residence when he was urgently summoned.

'Send for a good hakim. Quickly! The begum is not feeling well.'

'Ji Sarkar,' said Sheikh Chilli, hurrying to obey orders. Within a short time there appeared a hakim, a kafan maker, who stitches garments for the dead, as well as two gravediggers!

'What is all this?' demanded Chhotey Nawab angrily. 'No one is dead here. I only asked for a hakim. Who sent for the others?'

'I did, Sarkar!' said Sheikh Chilli. 'You said a good worker does far more than the work assigned to him. So I prepared for all eventualities. May Allah protect Begum Sahiba, but who knows what can happen in an illness!'

*

Chhotey Nawab did not pay much attention to the

affairs of the state. He preferred to spend his time hunting, or playing chess and other games. One day he decided to hold a contest to see who could tell the biggest lie! The winner, it was announced, would get a thousand gold coins!

Many 'liars' came forward, eager to win the prize. Said one, 'Sarkar, I have seen ants which are as big as buffaloes and give forty seers of milk at a time!'

'Why not?' said Chhotey Nawab. 'It's possible.'

'Sarkar, every night I fly to the moon and fly back before sunrise!' boasted another liar.

'Could be,' said Chhotey Nawab. 'You may possess some secret powers.'

'Sarkar,' said a fat man with a bulging stomach, 'ever since I swallowed the seeds of a watermelon, small watermelons have been growing inside my stomach. As each ripens, it bursts open and so I always have food in my stomach and don't need to eat anything else.'

'You must have swallowed some very powerful seeds,' observed Chhotey Nawab, without batting an eyelid.

'Sarkar, may I have permission to speak?' asked Sheikh Chilli.

'Certainly,' smirked Chhotey Nawab. 'What words of brilliance can we expect from you?'

'Sarkar,' said Sheikh Chilli loudly, 'the biggest fool

in this state is you! You do not deserve to be sitting on the Nawab's throne!'

There was a stunned silence in the court. Then Chhotey Nawab roared, 'Guards, arrest that man!'

Sheikh Chilli was caught and dragged in front of him.

'You rogue!' spluttered the infuriated Nawab, 'How dare you! Your head will be struck off if you don't fall at our feet this very instant and beg our pardon!'

'But Sarkar,' protested Sheikh Chilli, 'you said you wanted to hear the biggest lie!' He looked innocently at Chhotey Nawab. 'What could be a bigger lie than what I said?'

Chhotey Nawab was stumped! He did not know what to think. Was Sheikh Chilli lying now or had he lied earlier? Suddenly Sheikh Chilli did not seem to be as much of a fool as Chhotey Nawab had thought!

He smiled weakly and said, 'Shabash! You win the prize!'

Everyone praised Sheikh Chilli's ingenuity. He went home proudly with a thousand gold coins. Chhotey Nawab might be a bit of a fool, thought Sheikh, but he was a generous man!

The Capture

Once an ingenious robber entered the state of Jhajjar. He robbed both the rich and the poor and always managed to escape with his booty. Fear had gripped the people of the state. When even the Nawab's treasury was not spared, he sat up and took notice. A royal order was issued. Anyone who managed to catch the thief would be honoured by the Nawab and given enough wealth to live comfortably for the rest of his life.

But the one to remain unperturbed through all this drama was Sheikh Chilli. There was nothing in his house to attract a thief, Sheikh felt. Despite receiving a modest salary from the Nawab, Sheikh Chilli and his begum lived a fairly hand-to-mouth existence. Many times Sheikh Chilli forfeited part of his salary for daydreaming or some other foolishness at work. Whenever there was money in his pocket, he spent it with a happy and liberal heart, never forgetting those less fortunate than him.

One day Sheikh Chilli decided to seek the blessings of a well-known fakir in a neighbouring state. This meant he would be away from home for at least four days.

'Hai Allah! You are thinking of leaving me alone at such a time!' said his wife Fawzia. 'What if the thief decides to pay us a visit?'

'Begum, no thief will waste his time on us!' Sheikh assured her. 'Our neighbour's wife will stay with you at night till I return. And who knows, I may return with better luck for both of us!'

He left the following morning and returned a few days later with an amulet blessed by the holy man.

'The fakir said it would bring peace and prosperity to this house,' said Sheikh Chilli.

Fawzia took the amulet from him and pressed it reverentially to her eyes and lips. 'Inshallah!' she murmured.

After his meal, Sheikh Chilli went up to the terrace

of his house. Thousands of tiny stars twinkled in the dark night sky. As he paced up and down, many happy memories flooded his mind. Memories of his loving ammi, now dead; dim recollections of his abbu who had died when Sheikh was a toddler. He remembered the carefree days of his childhood, when he had flown kites from a roof much like this one. Sheikh Chilli began to dream … his kite was soaring higher and higher into the sky. Up! Up! Up! It went.

And down, down, down went Sheikh Chilli, right over the low terrace wall and down into the muddy lane with a thud and a yell of pain!

Luckily Sheikh escaped unhurt, except for a few bruises. He had not landed directly on the ground, but on a bundle of old clothes. As neighbours hurried to the spot with lanterns in their hands, the bundle of old clothes got up unsteadily and tried to run away! But he was caught and unmasked. The bundle of clothes was the thief who had been terrorising the state for so long! He had come to rob Sheikh Chilli, convinced that there must be wealth hidden in the house of a man who appeared so carefree!

The following day, the Nawab publicly commended Sheikh Chilli on the capture of the thief and confirmed that henceforth the royal treasury would take care of all of Sheikh Chilli's expenses.

The blessing of the amulet had worked!

Read more in the **Wise Men of the East** series from Scholastic:

The Wisdom of Mulla Nasruddin
Shahrukh Husain

In a small town somewhere in the Middle East lived Mulla Nasruddin. Mulla Nasruddin was famous for being a bit odd. He reacted to the follies of his fellow men and to the challenges of daily life—be it catching a runaway basket or celebrating the birth of a pot— in a manner that people found strange. But most wise men agreed that beneath the apparent foolishness of Mulla Nasruddin was a keen perception that cut straight to the truth.

This collection of twenty-five tales contains all the fun and wisdom that make the stories of Mulla Nasruddin so widely read and well loved.

Read more in the **Wise Men of the East** series from Scholastic:

The Wit of Tenali Raman
Devika Rangachari

Everyone agreed that Raman of Tenali was very clever. As a boy, he exasperated people with his mischief just as much as he impressed them with his intelligence. As jester in the court of Kind Krishna Devaraya, Tenali continued to entertain and annoy the king and courtiers in equal measure. But underlying the buffoonery and audacious exploits was a keen concern for truth and a desire to bring to light the follies of men and society.

This collection of eighteen stories contains all the wit and wisdom that make the stories of Tenali Raman so widely read and well loved.

Read more in the **Wise Men of the East** series from Scholastic:

Birbal the Clever Courtier
Anupa Lal

The cleverness of Birbal, the most famous minister in the Mughal emperor Akbar's court, is legendary.

Whenever Emperor Akbar had a problem to solve, or a philosophic question to ask, it was Birbal he turned to. And Birbal would provide him with thought-provoking or bizarre answers, which resolved the monarch's dilemma. So whether it was why the palms of people's hands are hairless, or if a mango tree could stand witness in court, or whether all sons-in-law should be hanged, Birbal could suggest an intelligent and funny solution to these problems. This made him Akbar's favourite, which in turn earned Birbal the envy of the other courtiers.

This collection of twenty-one fabulously funny stories contains all the wit and wisdom that make the stories of Birbal so widely read and loved.